As the curtain fell on *The Boy, The Bear, The Baron, The Bard*, I never quite knew what the Boy would get up to next. I left him wandering the streets of London. But somehow his irrepressible spirit has landed him in another amazing predicament. And he discovers that adventure can be found in the most unlikely of places.

I often wonder about the real lives of people in paintings. The older the painting, the more curious the people. I have long admired the paintings of Vermeer and Van Eyck and this book gave me the perfect opportunity to step inside and see for myself. Together the Boy and I discovered a mysterious world just beyond the gilded frame—a world of fun, friendship, and fiendish excitement.

GREGORY ROGERS

Praise for THE BOY, THE BEAR, THE BARON, THE BARD:

★ "Rogers's very funny wordless escapade . . . gets even better with rereading. With its harried pace and sportive sight gags—not to mention its undignified rendering of Shakespeare—this chase comedy proves to be a bravura performance."
–*Publishers Weekly* (starred review)

★ "The story is a rollicking chase, punctuated by a cozy nap for a boy and a bear and a merry dance later on when all fugitives hop on to Queen Elizabeth's barge . . .The good-humored action and touching friendships need no explanation. One-of-a-kind fun."
–*Kirkus Reviews* (starred review)

Praise for MIDSUMMER KNIGHT:

"This is another wordless adventure . . . that will delight young readers (and the young at heart). The climactic battle . . . is a visual feast of humor and action, and Shakespeare as a villain is an absolute hoot."
–*Booklist*

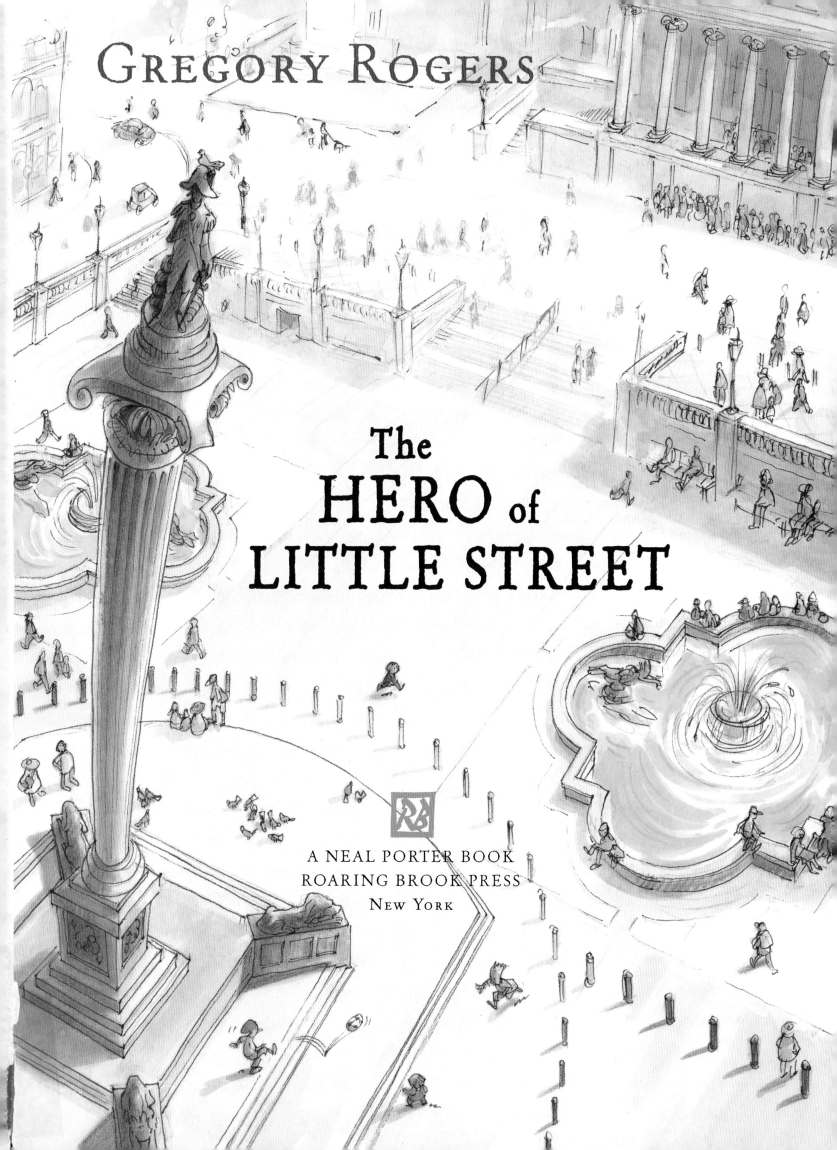

GREGORY ROGERS

The
HERO of
LITTLE STREET

A NEAL PORTER BOOK
ROARING BROOK PRESS
New York

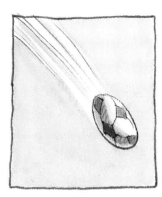

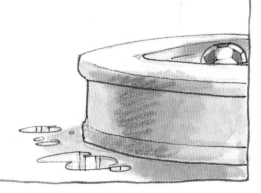

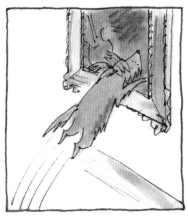

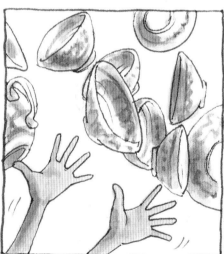

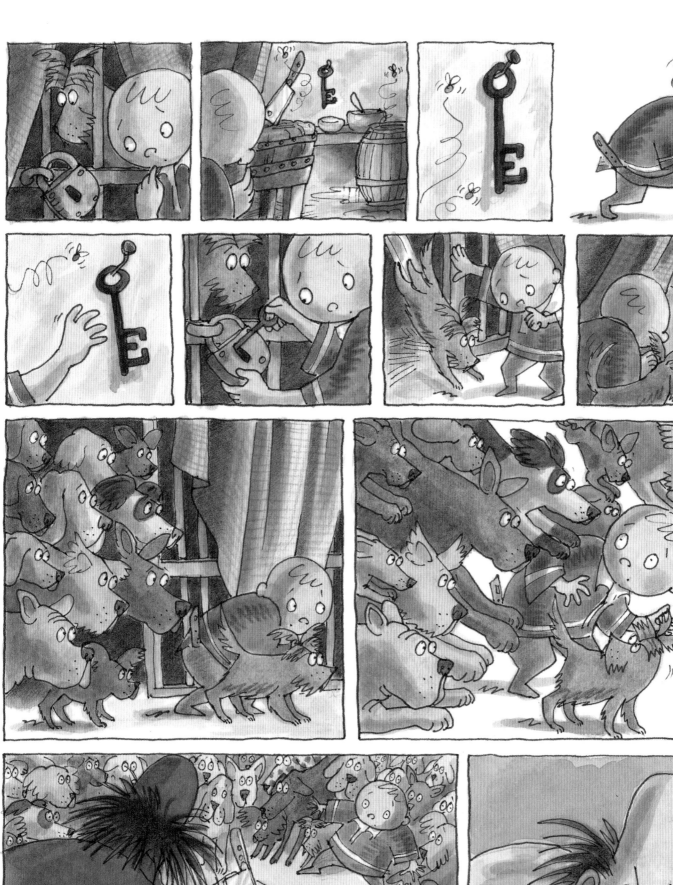

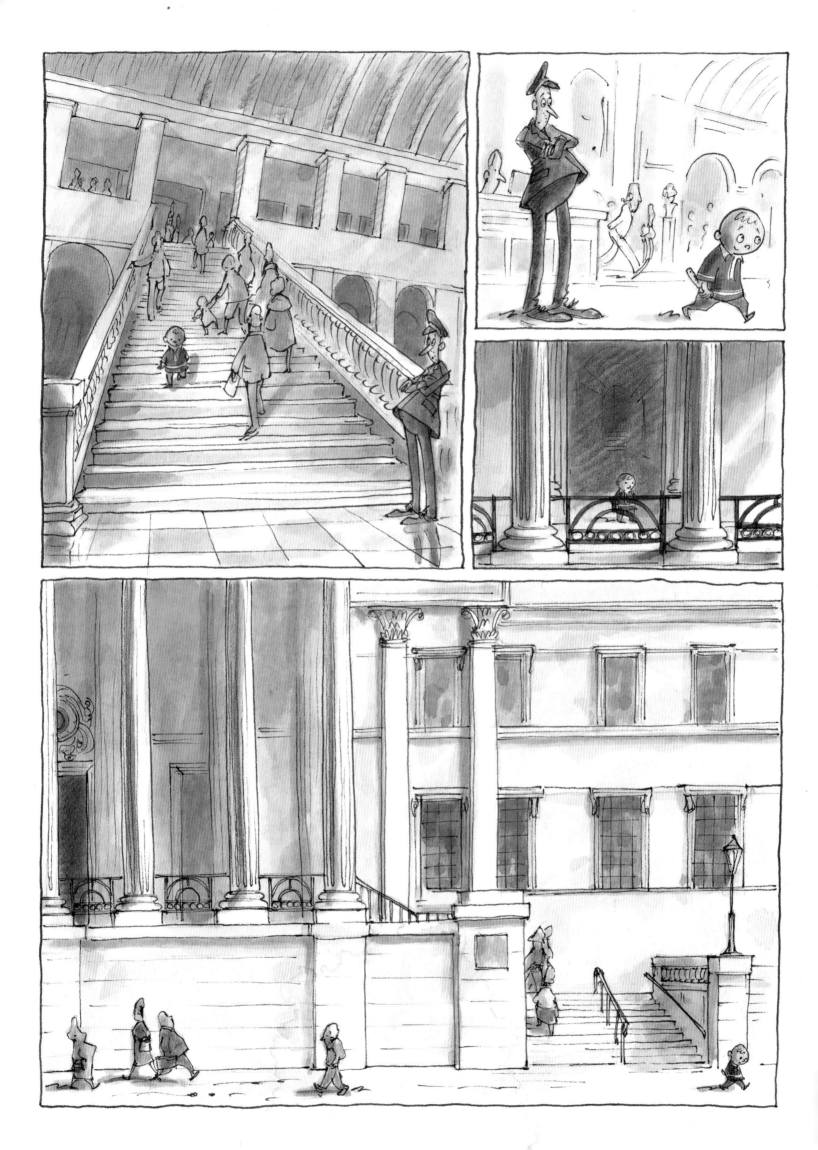

ACKNOWLEDGEMENTS

Thanks to the Boy who reignited my love of Jan Vermeer's world. And to the Arnolfinis whose dog always looked happier than they ever did. Thanks to Jodie Webster and Erica Wagner, my guardian angels; Margaret Connolly, the voice of reason and common sense; Neal Porter, whose quiet smile made the memory of all the hard work seem to melt away; and to my many friends and furry companions for just being there.

Library of Congress Cataloging-in-Publication Data
Rogers, Gregory.
    The hero of Little Street / Gregory Rogers. — 1st American ed.
        p.   cm.
    "A Neal Porter book."
    Summary: Chased through present-day London, a boy seeks refuge in the
National Gallery where a dog escapes from the painting of one Dutch master
and together they leap into the painting of another, where their adventures
in seventeenth-century Delft are a prelude to returning to London and
continuing the chase.
    ISBN 978-1-59643-729-6
    1. Stories without words. (1. Stories without words. 2. Dogs—Fiction.
3. Painting—Fiction. 4. Time travel—Fiction. 5. London
(England)—History—21st century—Fiction. 6. Great Britain—History—21st
century—Fiction. 7. Delft (Netherlands)—History—17th century—Fiction.
8. Netherlands—History—17th century—Fiction.) I. Title.

    PZ7.R62563Her 2012
    (E)—dc22

                                                        2010042371

Roaring Brook Press books are available for special promotions and premiums.
For details contact: Director of Special Markets, Holtzbrinck Publishers.

First published in Australia in 2009 by Allen & Unwin
First American Edition 2012
Book design by Gregory Rogers
Printed in December 2011 in China by Macmillan Production Asia Ltd.,
Kwun Tong, Kowloon, Hong Kong (supplier code 10)

1 3 5 7 9 8 6 4 2